The poison frog mystery.

Author: Gertrude Chandler Warner
RL 4.2
Points: 3.0
Accelerated quiz #36470

L6

The Boxcar Children® Mysteries

THE POISON FROG MYSTERY

created by
GERTRUDE CHANDLER WARNER

Illustrated by Charles Tang

ALBERT WHITMAN & Company
Morton Grove, Illinois

Library of Congress Cataloging-in-Publication Data

Warner, Gertrude Chandler, 1890-1979
The poison frog mystery/
created by Gertrude Chandler Warner;
illustrated by Charles Tang.
    p.   cm. — (The Boxcar Children mysteries)
Summary: The Aldens investigate when exotic and endangered animals
begin to disappear from the zoo where their new friend Lindsey works.
ISBN 0-8075-6586-5(hardcover)—
ISBN 0-8075-6587-3(paperback)
[1. Zoos—Fiction. 2. Endangered species—Fiction.
3. Brothers and sisters—Fiction. 4. Orphans—Fiction.
5. Mystery and detective stories.]
I. Tang, Charles, ill. II. Title.
III. Series: Warner, Gertrude Chandler, 1890-
Boxcar children mysteries.
PZ7.W244Po 2000   99-043097
[Fic]—dc21   CIP

Cover art by David Cunningham.

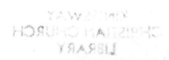

Contents

THE POISON FROG MYSTERY

CHAPTER 1

Something Is Definitely Wrong

Grandfather Alden drove slowly through the crowded parking lot, searching for an open space.

"There's one! There's one!" Benny cried.

Grandfather made a quick turn and slipped the car into the spot.

"Finally," the handsome gray-haired man said with a smile. "Nice going, eagle eyes." He patted six-year-old Benny on the knee.

The doors swung open and the Alden family filed out.

"I thought we'd never find a space," twelve-year-old Jessie said.

"It was getting so hot in there," Violet added, waving her hand in front of her face. At ten, she was the second youngest of the four Alden children.

Henry, the oldest at fourteen, said, "It's a perfect day for the zoo."

"It certainly is," Grandfather Alden said, looking up into the clear summer sky. "Is everybody ready?"

"Yeah!"

They started toward the entrance, Benny bounding ahead with excitement. The Aldens had spent many Saturdays at the Collingwood Zoo, but today was different. One of the zookeepers, Lindsey Taylor, was the niece of an old friend of Grandfather's. Today was the day her special project — an endangered-species breeding program—was to be opened to the public. The program was designed to allow rare animals to increase their numbers in the safety of the zoo, rather than in the more dangerous environments in the wild. When the babies were strong enough they would be released back into the wild in the hope that someday the animals wouldn't be so rare anymore. The program had been advertised in the local newspapers and on local television for months.

The children already knew what an endangered species was — a type of animal so rare, it was in danger of disappearing forever. Because the animals were so rare, the government didn't want zoos taking any of them from the wild. Every now and then, however, a zoo was allowed to capture a few in order to start a breeding program. Only the best zoos were chosen. When the Collingwood Zoo turned out to be one of them, it was a great honor for Lindsey.

There was a long line to get into the zoo, but it moved quickly. When they got to the ticket window, Grandfather took his wallet out of his back pocket and said, "One adult and four children, please."

"Have a nice visit," the woman said as she took the money and handed Grandfather the tickets. The children made sure to thank her as they walked in.

Stepping through the turnstile and onto the zoo's grounds was like stepping into another world. The very first thing they saw was a round fountain at the crest of a small green hill. In the center of the fountain stood a statue of two giant panda bears playing together.

"That's so cute!" Violet said, and she snapped a picture with the camera hanging from her neck.

"Grandpa? Can I have a giant panda bear someday?" Benny asked.

Grandfather mussed Benny's hair. "I don't think so, Benny. Giant panda bears are very rare. They're endangered, too. I don't think even this zoo is allowed to have them."

Benny considered this for a moment, then nodded. "Okay," he said. "I don't think Watch would want a giant panda bear as a friend anyway." Watch was the Aldens' family dog.

The others laughed. "Probably not,"

Henry agreed, putting his arm around his little brother.

They walked around the fountain, toward the sign that gave directions to all the zoo's many wonderful places. Before they were completely out of sight of the entrance and exit area, however, Grandfather and Henry both noticed something unusual—a pair of uniformed men carefully watching the people who were leaving the zoo. One of them stopped a woman and checked through a large bag she was carrying. Grandfather and Henry exchanged a glance. *What's that all about?* the look seemed to say.

The information sign was decorated in rainbow colors and the zoo exhibits were cleverly named: THE BIRD BARN, THE REPTILE RANGE, AMPHIBIAN HALL, and THE ELEPHANT HIDEAWAY. An arrow pointed the way to each exhibit.

Violet clicked a picture.

"You photographed the sign?" Grandfather asked.

"Yes. It's very colorful. I want to take a lot of pictures today. Anything that looks nice." This came as a surprise to no one. Violet was a very artistic young girl, with a keen eye for beautiful things. Often, after taking photographs, she would spend hours drawing pictures at home based on the photos she had taken.

"Grandfather, I want to go to the Elephant Hideaway!" Benny said, pulling on his grandfather's sleeve.

"Okay, Benny. We'll go to *all* the exhibits, I promise."

"I bet elephants eat a lot!" Benny exclaimed.

"Not as much as you do," Henry joked, and everyone—including Benny—laughed. It was no secret that the youngest Alden had the appetite of a bear. Benny always got teased about it, but he didn't mind. He was proud of his bottomless stomach!

Jessie patted him on the shoulder. "If you're good, I'll buy you an ice-cream cone," she told him. She sounded like a mom more than a sister. But that was Jessie —a little more grown-up than most twelve-year-olds.

And Henry, as the oldest boy, often acted like a father. Jessie and Henry felt responsible for their younger brother and sister. Their own parents had died some years ago, and for a short time they were orphans. They had no place to live, no food, and only a few belongings besides the clothes on their backs.

Then they discovered an abandoned boxcar deep in the woods near their old home, and they moved into it. Soon after that their grandfather, whom they had never met, arrived in town. But when they heard he was looking for them, they hid. They'd been told that he was mean and would treat them badly.

Because of this, Grandfather had to pretend he was someone else at first. He wanted the children to like and trust him. By the time he finally told them who he really was, they knew he wasn't mean at all. So they went back to live with him in Greenfield, Connecticut, where he had a beautiful house with a big backyard.

"Well, first things first," he told them on

this beautiful morning. "We should find Lindsey to let her know we're here. Besides, I think she wants to show us some things that the other visitors won't get to see. Some behind-the-scenes things."

"Really?"

"I believe so, yes. Now, where are the main offices?"

Violet pointed. "Look at the bottom of the sign."

The last line said HUMAN EXHIBITS (MAIN OFFICES), with an arrow pointing the way.

"Well, someone certainly has a sense of humor around here," Grandfather said. "Let's go."

The Aldens followed a winding path that led past a row of trees, some park benches, and a cluster of picnic tables. They came to a tall and stately old building that looked as though it had been recently repaired. It was built of white brick and had black shutters. The sign by the front door said MAIN OFFICES, and the door was wide open.

Stepping into the cool, sunlit hallway, the

Aldens found Lindsey's office. It was the second door on the left. The plaque read, LINDSEY AMANDA TAYLOR, ASSISTANT HEAD CURATOR.

"What's a cur . . . a . . . tor?" Benny asked.

"Someone who takes care of something," Jessie answered. "In this case, she takes care of the animals."

The door was open only a few inches, so Grandfather knocked.

"Lindsey? Are you in there?"

No answer.

He knocked again. "Lindsey, it's the Aldens!"

Still no answer. Grandfather checked his watch. "Hmmm, ten o'clock on the dot. That's odd."

"What's odd?" Violet asked, sounding worried.

"Lindsey's never late. She's always been very punctual."

Grandfather pushed the door back a little farther and he and the children peered inside. Lindsey's office was one large room, with a tall window on the right side and a desk on the left.

Lindsey wasn't at her desk, and there were signs that something was wrong.

"Look!" said Benny, pointing.

Lindsey's chair had been knocked over and was lying on the floor. Also, her phone was off the hook.

Grandfather stepped inside, the children following close behind.

"Something's not right," he said flatly.

Henry stepped behind Lindsey's desk and picked up the phone. A string of beeps came from the earpiece, meaning that the phone had been off the hook for some time. He also noticed a little red light on the phone labeled NEW MESSAGES. It was blinking wildly. "You're right, Grandfather," Henry said. "Something definitely isn't — "

At that moment, someone came running down the hallway and into the office.

"Lindsey!" Grandfather said, obviously alarmed. "What's the matter?"

Lindsey looked with surprise at James Alden and the children.

"Oh, Mr. Alden, something awful has happened!" She was clearly distracted and distressed and looked for a moment at her overturned chair. "I must have knocked this over when I got the news." She righted the chair and turned to face the Aldens. "Two of the animals from the breeding program have been stolen!" she said.

CHAPTER 2

The Missing Ferrets

Lindsey knew the Alden children had solved quite a few mysteries, so she brought them to the scene of the crime. It was a good-sized room in the small-mammal house. It was brightly lit, with a cement floor and pale yellow walls. A bank of cages lined the left side of the room along with a double sink with a hose, a large garbage can, and a long table. The wall to the right was filled by shelves of supplies, bags of food, and some cleaning chemicals. The faint scent of animals hung in the air.

Lindsey paced from the shelves to the sink and back again. She was obviously upset.

Grandfather had known her since she was a small child. She'd always loved animals, so it came as no surprise that she ended up working for a zoo. Eventually the Alden children got to know her, too. Jessie and Violet particularly admired her. She was tough and smart, and she stood behind the things she really believed in. Her sharp green eyes didn't miss anything, and she usually wore her long blond hair in a ponytail to keep it out of her face.

"They were in here," she told the Aldens, stopping at one of the cages. There was a little paper card in a slot on the door. It read, BLACK-FOOTED FERRETS. Under that, someone had written, TINA AND TIM. "They were going to be shown this morning," she added.

She crossed the room and unhooked a small brass latch on the wall. A broad panel dropped down. It looked like a secret door. "Take a look in here."

The Aldens came over and peered into a tiny landscape. There were sand, dead tree branches, tiny bushes, and piles of rocks. Inside one rock pile was a little pool of water. At the far end, in a dark corner, was a small hill with a hole in the center. The hole was about as wide as a baseball.

"This is *cool*!" Benny gawked. Suddenly being a zookeeper seemed like the greatest job in the world.

"Beautiful," Violet added. "And so real."

"I guess this is where Tina and Tim were supposed to go," Henry volunteered.

Lindsey nodded. "That's right. We were going to show them for the very first time today. But now . . ."

She pointed to the front of the enclosure. The glass had been covered by big sheets of brown paper. The Aldens could see the shadows of passing visitors on the other side. One of the zoo workers had written something on the paper. Although the words were backward, the Aldens could still tell what they said: THIS DISPLAY TEMPORARILY CLOSED. SORRY!

"Some of our visitors are going to be up-set!" she told them. "Black-footed ferrets are very rare. Some people have traveled a long way to see them. We're one of only three zoos in the world that has them!"

She went back over to their empty cage and closed the door. There was a bowl of water inside. It made the cage look emptier somehow.

"Is there any chance the ferrets got out on their own?" Jessie asked. "Maybe some-one forgot to lock it?"

Lindsey shook her head and took some-thing off the long table.

"No. Look at this."

She handed Jessie an ordinary lock — or-dinary except that it was all beaten up. It looked like it had been struck with some-thing very heavy, like a large rock or a brick.

"Someone definitely came in and broke that off the cage."

"Did they use something in here?" Henry asked, looking around the room.

"I don't think so," Lindsey answered.

"They probably brought something with them. A hammer, perhaps." She nodded in the direction of the supply shelves. "They also took a bag of food. One is missing, and we keep very careful track of how much we have. We need to, because we need to know how much the animals are eating."

"Which food did they take?" Violet asked.

"A bag for the herbivores," Lindsey answered. "Herbivores are the animals that eat plant matter, like berries and fruits and leaves."

Henry went over to the window that was still open. "I guess the thief came in here, right?"

"Probably. Only one window was unlocked when we checked; but then, the thief would've needed only one."

Just then the door opened and a young woman hurried in.

"Is it true, Lindsey, about the ferrets?" she asked.

"I'm afraid so, Beth," said Lindsey, and she introduced the young woman to the

Aldens. She explained that Beth was an intern at the zoo, helping the mammal keeper while going to college to learn to be a zookeeper herself. Beth looked to be in her early twenties, and instead of the usual green zoo uniform, she wore overalls covered with decorative patches that declared her love of animals. SAVE THE WHALES, EXTINCT MEANS FOREVER, and ANIMALS ARE PEOPLE, TOO, some of them stated.

She was clearly upset about the ferret theft. She suggested that perhaps the carelessness of the other keepers was to blame. "I hate to say it, Lindsey, but most of the people around here just don't take their jobs seriously enough," she was saying. "And no one takes their job as seriously as *I* do."

"I know you're upset, Beth, and that the ferrets were your special favorites. But we shouldn't go around wildly blaming one another. For now let's just stay calm and keep our eyes and ears open." Then, to gently change the subject, Lindsey asked, "Are the morning feedings finished yet?"

"Almost," Beth said, taking a bag of food

from the shelf. She gave Lindsey a meaningful look and added, "I'll let you know if I see anything suspicious," then left the room.

"She sure does care a lot about the animals!" said Benny. "I bet she'll make a good zookeeper someday."

"She *does* care a lot about animals, Benny," said Lindsey, "but if she is going to be a good zookeeper she will have to learn how to get along with *people* a little bit better. I'm afraid she thinks she knows more about animals than she really does — and that might keep her from learning more."

Upon hearing this, Jessie couldn't help but ask, "Do you think it's possible that because she loves the animals so much, and because she thinks no one else can care for them better than she can, maybe *she* took them? I mean, I don't want to go around accusing anyone already, but is it possible?"

Lindsey gave this some thought. "I guess it's *possible*. Anything's possible at this point." Then she shrugged. "But we'll see. Let's get some more evidence together before we start drawing conclusions. Now, where were we?"

"I was wondering what time you think the theft occurred," Grandfather said. "Do you have any idea?"

Lindsey shook her head. "It must have happened sometime between when we all left last night and when we came back in this morning. Aside from that . . ." She shrugged. "Who knows?"

"Maybe we could take a guess based on how much water the ferrets drank," Henry suggested.

Everyone looked at him, waiting for an explanation.

"How much water they drank," he said again. "If you know how much they usually drink during one night, we can figure it out from there. How much did you give them before you left, how much is there now, and how much do they usually drink in a night?"

Lindsey smiled — probably for the first time all day. "That's pretty clever."

"Good detectives need to be clever!" Benny told her.

"I'll have our head mammal keeper work on it," Lindsey went on. "I'll be seeing her later."

Violet shook her head. "But who would want to steal ferrets? Who would want to steal animals at all? That's so mean."

Lindsey said, "My guess is they stole the ferrets because they're valuable. Remember that they're a very rare species. There are only a few thousand black-footed ferrets left in the wild. There was a time, in fact, when scientists thought they *were* extinct. But then a little group of them was discovered. So they were almost all gone once before. We really can't afford to lose them again."

"But that still doesn't explain why they're valuable," Henry said. "Valuable to whom?"

Lindsey frowned. "You're never going to believe this, but . . . sometimes people buy rare animals to show them off, just to prove that they have them."

"Really?" Jessie asked.

"I'm afraid so. It doesn't happen a lot, but it *does* happen."

"That's awful," Violet said.

Henry crouched down, looking curiously at some little dents in the otherwise smooth cement floor. "Do these have anything to do with the theft?" He ran his hand over them. The surface of the floor was cold. "Were they here yesterday?"

"No," Lindsey answered. "The mammal keeper noticed them, too. She's sure they weren't there before. But no one has a clue as to how they got there or why."

"The thief could've dropped something heavy," Jessie suggested. "No one would've heard it."

Lindsey nodded. "I suppose that's possible."

"How many people knew the ferrets were here?" Grandfather asked.

"Not many," Lindsey answered quickly. "We were very careful about that. We wanted to advertise the breeding program, but we certainly didn't want to make a big deal about where exactly the animals were

being kept until today. There was no reason to."

"I noticed the zoo guards searching people's bags at the exit when we first came in," Henry mentioned.

"Yes, I noticed them, too," said Grandfather.

"Actually, they're not zoo guards," Lindsey told them. "They're the local police."

"The police!" Violet exclaimed.

"Uh-huh." Lindsey let out a long, weary sigh. "Boy, are we ever going to be in trouble if we don't get those ferrets back. Big trouble."

Jessie went over and put her hand on Lindsey's shoulder. "Don't worry, we'll help you find them."

"Of course we will," Violet said.

"That's right," Henry added.

"Hasn't been a mystery yet we couldn't solve!" Benny assured her.

Lindsey smiled. "I hope this one isn't any different," she said.

Then her smile disappeared again.

After the hectic day, Lindsey invited the Aldens back to her apartment for dinner. Grandfather Alden politely declined because he wanted to get some rest. He had a busy week of business ahead. Fortunately, Lindsey's apartment was only a few blocks away from home, so the children were allowed to go without him.

After dinner Lindsey showed the children her huge collection of nature books and the dozens of colorful paintings and photographs on her living room walls. Some were animal pictures but others showed plants, particularly flowers.

After talking all day about the stolen ferrets, Lindsey was ready for more cheerful topics. So she told the children stories about funny things that had happened to her at the zoo. She started with one about a koala bear. The keeper had forgotten to lock the cage, and it found its way out. It was missing for three days, and for a while the zoo thought they'd never find it again. Then a woman visitor stopped by Lindsey's office and told her how much she liked the "live outdoor exhibits in the lunch area." Lindsey was speechless — the zoo didn't *have* any live outdoor exhibits in the lunch area! Hurrying to the scene, she discovered the koala in a small tree. About a dozen visitors were standing around it, taking pictures.

When listening to Lindsey's funny story, Violet looked at the gorgeous framed pictures and the books. Certainly there were more beautiful pictures in each of them! Lindsey told Violet she could look through any book she wanted.

When she spotted a book about small mammals, she thought of the black-footed ferrets. Sure enough, there was a section on ferrets at the back. Violet looked through it and was surprised at how much she already knew about black-footed ferrets from what Lindsey had told them today:

Adults weigh about a pound and a half. . . . They live in burrows and are very secretive. . . . Light brown with black markings on their feet, giving them their name . . .

She kept reading, hoping maybe she'd come across something she didn't know. It didn't take long, and when she got to that information, her heart jumped:

Black-footed ferrets are carnivores, which means they eat meat.

"Oh, no," she said to herself.

"What's the matter, Violet?" Jessie asked.

"Huh? Oh, nothing, sorry." She didn't want to bring up the ferrets again, at least not today. She knew Lindsey was tired of talking about them.

But she still looked worried, and Lindsey noticed this. "C'mon, Violet. What's up?"

"Um, well . . . I don't mean to bring this up again, but I read something here about the black-footed ferrets, and I don't know if it's important or not."

"What's it say?"

"It says that they only eat meat. They're carnivores."

"So?" Henry asked.

"You mentioned that the thief stole a bag of food. That was food for — "

"Herbivores!" Lindsey said.

"What are herbivores again?" Benny asked.

"Herbivores are plant-eaters," Lindsey told him. "They only eat plant leaves, berries, nuts, and stuff like that."

"So if the thief took only a food bag for a herbivore," Jessie cut in, "then that means — "

"That means the ferrets don't have anything to eat," Lindsey said in almost a whisper.

"Will they . . . will they get sick?" Benny asked timidly.

"I don't think so," Lindsey replied. "If you had gone to the trouble of stealing them, wouldn't you make sure you knew how to take proper care of them? As soon as they see that the ferrets won't eat any of the stolen food, they'll probably check a book for more information. Just like you did."

The children still looked worried about the ferrets' health.

"Look," Lindsey said, "whoever stole the ferrets obviously cares about them. If the thief didn't care, he or she wouldn't have bothered to take any food at all. Please don't worry. They'll be all right."

"Well, at least we have another little clue to build on," Jessie said.

"What's that?"

"The thief doesn't know what ferrets eat."

This *was* a little clue. It certainly ruled out the possibility that one of the more experienced zookeepers in the mammal house was the thief.

"Good point," Lindsey said. "Very good point."

CHAPTER 3

Partners

The next morning Lindsey had a meeting with Jordan Patterson, one of the zoo's two owners. They planned to meet in the ferret room at noon. Lindsey knew \the Aldens planned to see the rest of the zoo that morning, so she asked them to stop by afterward so they could meet Jordan.

As soon as the Alden children arrived at the zoo, they split up: Violet and Jessie went to the Bird Barn, while Henry and Benny stopped at the Reptile Range.

The first floor of the Reptile Range was

filled with exhibits of snakes and lizards. On the second floor they saw turtles and alligators. On the third and final floor was Amphibian Hall, where the zoo kept all the amphibians. Here Benny and Henry looked at frogs, toads, salamanders, and newts from all over the world.

Benny thought snakes and lizards were neat. He was fascinated by all the different colors and patterns, and by how some snakes were so tiny while others were huge. Some were poisonous while others were harmless.

Benny played a game with himself — he made a list in his head of his favorite snakes and lizards. He saw some pretty scarlet snakes and a shiny black indigo snake. Once they had seen all the snakes, Benny decided his favorites were the beautifully striped red, white, and black San Francisco garter snakes.

He turned to tell Henry he had chosen his favorite, then stopped. The young man standing next to him wasn't Henry! Benny was surprised and embarrassed and a little bit afraid. He turned quickly, all around, until he spotted Henry on the other side of the room still gazing at the scarlet snakes. Benny had been so interested in the animals that he hadn't noticed he'd walked so far away from his brother. He hadn't even heard the young man next to him come into the room. It was as if he had just appeared.

The young man had his hands deep in his jacket pockets, Benny noticed, and he stared into the enclosure with a hint of a smile on his lips. He was standing perfectly still, Benny thought, as if he'd fallen asleep with his eyes open. Even from the side, Benny could tell the young man had unusually bright blue eyes. Another thing Benny noticed was the Boston Red Sox baseball cap. It was easy to recognize — red with a blue B at the front. But it was hard to get a better look at him without being rude.

"Aren't these beautiful animals?" the stranger asked. He looked and sounded like an older teenager, or maybe twenty at most.

"Er . . . yeah, they really are. And rare, too. They're part of the zoo's endangered-

species program!" Benny liked to hear himself use such big words.

The young man nodded. "I know. I've been following the story in the newspapers. Boy, would I love to have an animal collection like this. I love reptiles and amphibians most of all, but I love all animals, really. They're doing really wonderful things here at the zoo."

"They sure are. Snakes are my favorite," Benny said.

"Are they?"

"Yeah, although I like all animals a lot."

The stranger nodded. "So do I. I like everything about nature. The animals, the plants, the fresh air."

"Me, too," Benny replied.

The young man never took his eyes off the snakes, never really moved a muscle.

"Well, have a nice day," Benny said finally.

"You, too."

Benny turned away to look for Henry. The young man seemed friendly enough, but Grandfather wouldn't have been very happy if Benny spent too much time talking to strangers.

Just then Benny's eye was caught by some movement in the next enclosure. It was a fat brown cricket scuttling up a low branch. A chameleon was nestled in some leaves high above, watching it carefully. Then, in a flash, the chameleon fired its long tongue out and brought the cricket back into its mouth. *Wow*, Benny thought. *That was unbelievable!*

Unable to control his excitement, he turned back toward the young man and said, "Did you see that?"

But the stranger had disappeared, again without making a sound. It almost seemed like he hadn't ever really been there at all.

Benny shivered. Then he hurried over to Henry.

Ten o'clock rolled around, and Lindsey and the Aldens met with Jordan Patterson in the same room where the ferrets had been stolen.

The Aldens liked Jordan from the moment they met him. He was a tall, thin man in his mid-thirties. He had short brown hair and a round, pleasant face. He also smiled a lot. Lindsey had told the Aldens on the way over that he was one of the gentlest, kindest, and most caring people she'd ever met. Never once, she said, had she ever seen him lose his temper or even raise his voice. She also said that he was a genius when it came to animals. That was probably why he was the head curator of the zoo as well as part owner.

"We love your zoo, Mr. Patterson," Jessie told him when she shook his hand. "It's really wonderful."

"Thank you, Jessie," he replied. "It's a pleasure having you and the rest of your family as our guests. And please call me Jordan."

"Okay, Jordan."

Violet said, "It's really terrible what happened to your black-footed ferrets."

Jordan sighed and ran a hand through his hair. "I'm very worried about those two. I hope they're okay."

"Did Lindsey tell you about the food?" Henry asked.

"Yes, she did. Thank you for noticing that."

"Thank Violet," Henry said. "She's the one who noticed."

Jordan nodded. "Lindsey tells me you're all pretty good detectives."

"We like to help when we can," said Jessie.

"Well, I'd appreciate any help. We've really got to get those animals back."

"Have the police started any kind of investigation?" Henry asked.

"We've spoken to them and they are going to let us do as much as we can on our own right now. I don't want any bad news about the zoo to get into the papers." Jordan shrugged. "Who knows? Maybe the solution to the mystery is very simple. We'll see."

The door to the hallway opened, and an older man in a dark suit walked in. He was a large, imposing figure, with carefully trimmed silver hair, deeply tanned skin, and a glittering gold watch.

"Jordan, my friend," he said in a deep voice, "how are you today?"

"Fine, Darren, and you?"

"Fine, just fine, thanks."

"Kids," Jordan said to the Aldens, "this is Mr. Colby, the other owner of the zoo. He's my partner."

The Aldens said polite hellos.

"Hello, kids. Are you having a good time at the zoo?"

"I am," Benny said. "I went to the Reptile Range this morning and picked out a fav — "

"That's great, just great," Mr. Colby said. "And how are you today, Linda?"

Lindsey put on a little smile and nodded. "Fine, Mr. Colby."

"Good for you. Uh, Jordan, may I have a word with you in the hallway, please?"

"Hmmm? Oh, sure. Excuse me for a moment, everyone."

The two men stepped out of the room, closing the door most of the way behind them.

"He called you Linda!" Jessie said to Lindsey in a whisper.

"At least it starts with an *L* now. Last month I was Nancy."

"You work for him and he doesn't even know your name?"

"He hardly knows anyone around here. He doesn't spend a lot of time at the zoo."

"That's strange," Jessie said.

"Not as strange as you might think," Lindsey replied. "Anyway, I talked to the head mammal keeper this morning while you guys were walking around. She noticed the same thing that you did, Violet, about the missing bag of food being the wrong kind. She's very upset, like everyone else."

"Does the mammal keeper suspect someone?" Henry asked.

"Well, she has never gotten along with Beth, the intern you met before. She thinks maybe Beth likes the ferrets *too* much."

"Enough to steal them?"

"I really don't think so, but I suppose we

can't rule her out as a suspect. She may have felt — mistakenly — that the ferrets would get better care with her. She's got all kinds of unusual pets — lizards, giant insects, even a monkey."

Benny wandered over to where the broken cage lock was still lying on the long table. He picked it up and started playing with it, then he looked into the empty ferret cage. He thought about the ferrets, where they were and whether they were doing okay. He wondered what kind of a person would steal animals from a zoo.

Suddenly he heard an angry voice through the crack in the door. It was Darren Colby, standing with Jordan Patterson in the hallway.

"I don't care what it takes!" Mr. Colby said sharply. "I want those animals found and brought back here!"

"I know you do, Darren," Jordan was saying. "So do I."

"Those animals were expensive!"

Benny didn't like that the ferrets were being talked about that way. It was as if Mr.

Colby thought of them as something he'd bought at the supermarket.

"Okay, Darren, take it easy," Jordan was saying in a calm, soothing voice. "We'll find them and everything will be fine."

"I don't want to have to hire a security guard," Mr. Colby said. "That's just more money down the drain! But I'll do it if I have to. And if any more animals disappear . . . well, you know."

There was a pause. Benny waited.

"Darren," Jordan said finally. "Shutting down the breeding program isn't going to solve anything. All it's going to do is make some rare animals even rarer. If we keep it going, we can save some of them from extinction."

"Saving them from extinction is costing us a lot of money!" Mr. Colby hissed.

"You'll make it all back, and more," Jordan assured him. "I promise."

Benny walked away from the door and rejoined the others. They had stopped talking about the investigation, and Lindsey was now telling them another funny story.

Something about a bear cub that was stealing visitors' lunches.

Benny wasn't really listening, though. Suddenly he didn't feel too well.

Lindsey and the Aldens went to the zoo's outdoor food court for lunch. It was a warm, shady area with round picnic tables and giant potted plants.

They sat at one of the tables and talked with Lindsey about some of the other animals the zoo wanted to keep in the future. "We don't want to focus entirely on endangered species," she said. "We'd also like to keep a few unusual animals. Animals that most people have never heard of. Every zoo in the world has monkeys, parrots, and elephants. We want to show some really strange animals, the kind that you don't normally see in zoos, books, or even on television."

"You should keep some unusual insects," Jessie suggested. "Zoos never do that."

Lindsey nodded. "We've thought about that. There are some pretty peculiar ones that I'll bet people would like, especially kids. In Mexico there are hissing cockroaches the size of your hand."

Jessie shivered. "I wouldn't like to see them."

"Yes, you would," Lindsey argued, smiling. "You couldn't help but look. You'd want to look *because* they're so gross."

Jessie laughed. "You're probably right."

"What about you, Benny?" Lindsey asked. "What weird animals would you like to see?"

The youngest Alden didn't seem to have heard the question. He was hovering over his plate, face pushed up on one hand, playing with a french fry.

"Benny?" Violet asked. "Are you okay?"

"Yeah."

He dropped the french fry and took a tiny sip of his milk shake.

"You can't be *that* okay," Jessie said. "You haven't touched your lunch."

"When Benny doesn't eat," Henry said to Lindsey, "you know something's wrong."

He moved over next to his little brother and put an arm around him. "C'mon, tell us what's bothering you."

"Well, I was thinking . . . maybe the zoo should just get animals that don't cost a lot of money. That way Mr. Colby won't get so mad."

Lindsey looked confused. "Mad? What do you mean, Benny?"

Benny reluctantly told them about the argument between Mr. Colby and Jordan Patterson that he'd overheard.

"I didn't mean to hear them," he pointed out. "I was just standing over by the door, looking at that banged-up lock."

Jessie said, "Of course you didn't mean it. No one thinks you'd do something like that on purpose."

"Okay, look," Lindsey said, "I know Mr. Colby doesn't sound like the sweetest man in the world. He certainly didn't go out of his way to make a great impression on you guys, either. But . . ." She studied one of the giant potted plants for a moment. "He's necessary. He's not an animal person, he's a money person. Do you understand what that means?"

The children shook their heads.

"It was hard for me to understand when I first came here, but after a while it made more sense. This zoo is a business, whether we like it or not. And in order for a business to survive, it has to make more money than it spends. Jordan is an animal expert. He isn't really much of a businessperson, so he needs Mr. Colby to keep an eye on the money side of things. It's Mr. Colby's *job* to think more about the money than about the animals."

Benny said, "After hearing him talk, I think I know what you mean by that."

"If the zoo didn't make money, we couldn't afford to feed all the animals, keep them in clean cages, and keep them warm in the winter. Doing all that costs money. Also" — Lindsey smiled and pointed to herself — "I wouldn't have a job. They wouldn't be able to pay me."

"That wouldn't be good!" Benny exclaimed.

"No, it wouldn't. And believe me, we certainly wouldn't be able to have a breeding program without money. That whole thing was very expensive to set up."

The Aldens nodded as they began to understand.

"Jordan and Mr. Colby get along," she continued. "They're not the best of friends, but they make a good team. They need each other to made the zoo work."

"I guess that's good," Jessie said.

Lindsey took a sip of her soda and put on a new smile. "So do you feel better now, Benny?"

The youngest Alden nodded. "Yes, much better."

"Are you sure?"

Benny looked at her curiously. "Mmm-hmmm. Why?"

"Because your burger still hasn't been touched."

Benny grabbed it and took a huge bite. The others laughed.

"So, would you all like to know about

our next secret breeding project?" Lindsey asked.

"Can you really tell us?" Violet replied.

"I think I can trust you guys. Our next endangered species will be . . . the California condors."

"You're kidding!" Jessie said.

"Nope. We'll be one of only four zoos in the world to have them."

"I saw a magazine article about them a few months ago," Jessie told her. "They're really rare."

Lindsey nodded. "There are only about a hundred left in the whole world, and all of them live in zoos. The long-term plan, though, is to put some back into the wild. We hope there will be thousands of them in the wild again someday."

"When are you getting them?" Henry asked.

"We've got them already. We're going to put them on display in about a week. For now, however, we're trying to get them used to their new surroundings. We've got them in the Bird Barn, in room number seven."

Lindsey told them about the California condors. As she spoke, Benny noticed a short, muscular young man sitting nearby, wearing a brightly colored checkered shirt and sunglasses. He was writing on a little notepad and seemed to be listening to their conversation. When Lindsey was done, the man got up and hurried away. Benny was going to say something, but then he realized he hadn't finished his french fries.

CHAPTER 4

The Jammed Window

Jessie and Henry were at home fixing breakfast for everyone when the phone rang. Henry was trying to balance four plates of bacon and eggs at the same time, so Jessie answered it after wiping her hands on her apron.

"Hello?"

"Jessie?" It was Lindsey, and she sounded frantic.

"Lindsey? What's wrong?"

"The California condors are missing!"

"Missing? You mean they've—"

"Yes, I'd appreciate it if you could all come down as soon as you can!" Lindsey said.

Then the line went dead.

The Alden children gobbled up their breakfast and rushed down to the zoo on their bicycles.

They found Lindsey in one of the back rooms of the Bird Barn. It looked similar to the back room in the mammal house, except for a huge enclosure at one end that had been made by closing off part of the room with long strips of wood and lots of chicken wire.

"That was where they were," Lindsey said. "Up until last night."

The floor of the cage was bedded with sand, wood chips, and huge rocks. In the center was a small tree. There were no leaves on it, just bare branches. It sort of looked like a giant hand reaching for the ceiling.

"The same person did it?" Jessie asked.

Lindsey nodded. She looked as though she were trying to fight back tears.

"I'm sure," she said. "We found the lock on the floor, all broken up. It's on that table over there if you want to look at it. The door to the cage was wide open when the birdkeeper came in. And that window back there . . ." she said, pointing toward the other end of the room, "that's where the thief came and went. The latch is broken. And another bag of food is missing. The right kind this time. I checked."

Benny picked up the broken lock and began examining it. It looked pretty much the same as the last one — mangled and beaten. There was some chalky dust on the corners, which he wiped away. This dust made him think of the special dust detectives use to find fingerprints. He wished he had some of that right now.

Henry went over to the window and pushed it open. The latch, just like Lindsey said, had been broken. *Whoever broke it must have been very strong or used a very forceful tool*, he thought, *because it was made of steel.*

He noticed that the window could be opened, but not by much. Only about eight or nine inches, in fact. Then it sort of got stuck.

"Lindsey, the thief really came and left through this window? Are you sure?"

"Positive," she said. "The lock wasn't broken yesterday. In fact, Jordan and Mr. Colby issued a strict order after the black-footed ferrets were stolen for everyone to make sure the windows were locked tight before they went home. The head bird-keeper swears he locked that window. If it hadn't been locked, why would the thief break the latch?"

Henry frowned. "That's not what puzzles me. It's the size of the opening."

"What do you mean?"

Henry pushed the window up as far as it would go. Then he put his hand through the opening.

"Look at how little room there is here. This window seems to be jammed." Henry tried opening it all the way, but it wouldn't budge. "Wouldn't the person who slipped through it have to be incredibly thin?"

"Yes, of course. That's a good point!" Lindsey said. "Some of these windows tend to jam up like that."

Benny, still playing with the broken lock, said, "I'm only six years old, and I don't think I could fit through there!"

"But someone must have," Violet added. "Unless . . . the thief broke in somewhere else."

Lindsey shook her head. "No, we've looked. No other signs of forced entry anywhere."

Violet also thought maybe the thief had a key, but that couldn't be possible, could it? Would someone who worked here actually do something like that? Wouldn't it be too obvious? She tucked the idea in the back of her mind for the time being.

"What does 'forced entry' mean?" Benny asked.

"This," Henry answered, pointing to the broken latch, "is forced entry. And so is that," he continued, pointing to the broken lock in Benny's hand. "When you have to *force* your way in, that's forced entry."

"Oh," Benny nodded. "I get it."

"*And*," Henry said, turning back to the window and putting his hands on his hips, "how could anyone fit two California condors through an opening that size? Aren't they big birds?"

"Yes, they are, but it can be done. Birds are, unfortunately, very 'squeezable.' That's why magicians use doves in their magic tricks — they can be squished into tiny places."

"That doesn't sound very nice," Violet said.

"If it's done gently it doesn't really hurt them," Lindsey quickly pointed out, "but I'm sure the birds aren't too happy. If the thief did that with the condors, I'll bet he or she had to fight with them. Condors are mean, tough birds. The thief probably got a fair share of bites and scratches."

They walked back over to the empty enclosure. "What about these little dents on the floor?" Jessie asked, pointing. There were maybe a dozen of them, all small and close together, a few feet from the cage door. "Same as last time?"

Lindsey nodded. "Exactly the same. And still just as puzzling."

Jessie knelt down and gently ran her hand over them.

"Just like in the mammal house," she said softly.

"Right," Lindsey said, "and they weren't here before the theft. I asked the head bird-keeper, just to be sure."

Henry said, "I wonder if they were caused by the thief's shoes. Maybe the thief was wearing cleats, or those shoes that mountain climbers use. They have spikes on the bottom."

"I doubt it," Lindsey replied. "If that were the case, why wouldn't the marks be all over the floor? Why only in one spot?"

Henry nodded. "That's true. I can't really think of anything else, though."

"Me neither," Lindsey said.

Jordan Patterson walked in at that moment, hands deep in the pockets of his jeans.

"Any good news, Jordan?"

He shook his head. "No news at all. Same as last time. I have to admit, whoever the thief is, he or she is very good; left no clues, no trail, nothing." He turned to the Aldens. "How are you kids coming along with your own investigation? Anything turn up?"

Henry told Jordan about his thoughts on the open window.

"That makes a lot of sense," Jordan said. "I'll mention that if and when the police get involved. Good point."

"Thanks," Henry said. "Does Mr. Colby know yet?"

Jordan frowned. "Yeah, I just finished talking to him."

"I assume he didn't take it too well?" Lindsey asked.

Jordan smiled at her, but there was no happiness in it. "No, he didn't. In fact, he was downright furious. He said he was going to hire a night guard. He has a friend whose son has guard experience. He's pretty good, from what I've heard."

"Well, that should help," Jessie said.

"I guess," Jordan replied. "It's a shame we have to go this far. Having a guard . . ." He shook his head. "This is a zoo, not a prison."

"But these thefts won't make us look very good to the public," Lindsey told the Aldens. "They'll make us look irresponsible and careless."

"Darren must think the same thing," Jordan said to Lindsey, "because he said something else, too."

"Oh?"

"He said he was going to shut down the breeding program if one more animal was taken." Jordan put up a finger. "Just one."

Lindsey's face paled. "You're kidding."

"No, I'm not. And I'm not surprised, either. He's been very worried about the possible response from the newspapers."

"But what about the endangered animals?" Violet asked.

Jordan shook his head. "I guess another zoo will have to take them."

"Oh, no!"

Jordan shrugged. "What else can we do? We can't risk losing any more of them."

He turned back toward the door. "Okay, I have to go back and talk to him again. Keep up the good work, kids."

"Thanks," Henry said.

"I hope they catch the thief soon," Lindsey said sadly after Jordan had gone. "Or we do, or someone does. Shutting down the program is going to be a huge blow to this zoo."

"Well, let's keep looking around for more clues," Henry said. "Who knows? The key piece to the whole puzzle might be right in this room."

"Maybe," Lindsey said, but she didn't sound as enthusiastic as Henry.

Henry went back to the window, Benny investigated the supply shelves, and Violet searched around inside the condors' empty cage.

Jessie, on the other hand, knelt down beside the dents in the floor again. There was something about them that seemed important to her—something way in the back of her mind. She could *feel* that they fit into the picture, but she couldn't quite figure out *how*.

She would, though, very soon.

It was early afternoon, and Violet and Benny were standing in Amphibian Hall. After the Aldens finished examining the room where the condors had been stolen, they had lunch, then decided to see the rest of the zoo before returning home. Benny insisted that Violet see the frog display.

Inside a huge glass-fronted enclosure were some of the most beautiful tropical plants Violet had ever seen, with huge green leaves attached to thick vines and branches. A little pipe that ran across the ceiling sprayed a fine mist of water. There were rocks and bubbling water pools, and even a tiny waterfall. It was perfect, Violet thought, even without the animals.

But the animals were what Benny had insisted she must see—and Violet was happy he had. They were frogs, but not like any other she'd ever seen. Most of them were so small they looked more like large bugs. One was blue and black, another was red and blue. A third was black and orange. One was a very bright yellow, and a few were a pure royal blue. These were the ones that took Violet's breath away.

"Benny, they're unbelievable!"

Her little brother smiled proudly. "I th ught you'd like them."

"I certainly do."

She read the information plaque on the wall. It said that these amphibians were called poison-arrow frogs, named because natives of South America used to coat the tips of their arrows with the poison that covered the frogs' skin. In spite of the frogs' small size, the poison was strong enough to cause severe rashes and other painful skin irritations in humans.

"Wow," Violet whispered. She was

amazed at how animals so beautiful could be so dangerous at the same time.

Benny and Violet decided to get a snack after seeing the rest of Amphibian Hall. They walked to the outdoor food court and chose a table in a patch of shade to sit and share an order of french fries. Benny was happily munching away when someone familiar caught his eye. A strongly built young man wearing sunglasses and a brightly colored flowered shirt had made his way off the paved walkway that wound between the exhibit houses. He was standing on tiptoe behind some bushes, peering into back rooms of the Bird Barn.

"Violet," said Benny, "look at that guy over there peeking into the Bird Barn. I'm pretty sure I've seen him at the zoo before. . . . Wouldn't it be much easier for him to see the birds if he just went inside to the exhibit?"

"You're right, Benny, but I don't think he is an ordinary zoo visitor. Look, he's taking notes."

The young man had flipped open a notebook and was writing in it. Then he seemed to be startled by a noise coming from the other side of the Bird Barn window. He looked around quickly, flipped his notebook closed, and hurried away.

Benny looked thoughtfully down at his french fries. "*Now* I remember," he said excitedly. "I did see him here before. When we ate lunch with Lindsey and she explained to us all about the California condors. He seemed to be listening to Lindsey and he was taking notes then, too!"

Violet and Benny looked at each other.

"Do you think we found another suspect?" asked Benny.

"I think so," answered Violet, "but who is he?"

CHAPTER 5

"Unlocking" the Mystery

The children returned home late that afternoon. After dinner they went into the living room with their grandfather to talk about everything that had been happening.

"I'll bet Lindsey's very upset," Grandfather said.

"She is, I can tell," Jessie replied. She and Violet were sitting together on one of the couches. Violet was drawing something in her sketch pad.

"And what about that Jordan Patterson

fellow you've been telling me about?" Grandfather added. "How's he doing?"

"I think he's upset, too," Henry answered. "The investigation is keeping him from spending more time with the animals, and I'm sure he doesn't like that very much."

"It's so unfair," Jessie added. "Whoever the thief is, I'm sure there's no good reason for what he or she has done. And to do it to people like Jordan and Lindsey is just terrible."

"Any new pieces to add to the puzzle?" Grandfather asked.

"Violet and I discovered a new piece to the puzzle," Benny piped up, "but we don't know how it fits in."

"And what's that?" Grandfather asked.

Benny and Violet went on to tell the others all about the suspicious young man they'd seen taking notes at the Bird Barn window.

"Hmmm," said Henry. "Taking notes. . . . You're right, Benny. We've definitely got another piece to the puzzle. Let's all keep a lookout for him at the zoo. Maybe it's more innocent than it appears. Or maybe he's the thief and he's planning another theft."

"If I were a thief," Violet said quietly, "I wouldn't wear such colorful shirts. They're not good for sneaking around."

"Have Lindsey and Jordan come up with any more information?" Grandfather asked.

Henry shook his head. "No, but we've discovered a few things." He went over the bit about the window possibly being too narrow for a normal-sized person to pass through, the missing bag of food from the mammal house, and the mysterious little dents on the floor. "But who knows if any of that stuff is important?"

"Well, I'm sure Jordan and Lindsey are very happy you kids are trying to help out in the first place. And I'm happy, too. I'm very proud of all of you."

"Mr. Colby is hiring a night guard," Jessie put in. "That should help, I guess."

Pausing between pencil strokes, Violet added, "Jordan wasn't too happy about it.

He said it made the zoo seem more like a prison."

"Maybe so," Grandfather told her, "but as Jessie said, it should help. If I were a thief, I'd think twice before breaking into a place that had a security guard."

"Mr. Colby doesn't really like the idea that much, though," Henry said, "because it's going to cost the zoo more money. He wasn't too thrilled about that."

"He's very money-minded," Jessie added. "That's what Lindsey said."

Grandfather nodded. "Well, every business needs someone like that. Without him, the zoo might not even exist." Grandfather laughed. "He's going to go broke buying new locks for the cages before anything else."

Benny, who had been playing on the carpet with Watch, looked up. "Why's that, Grandfather?"

"Because the thief is breaking them all, right?"

Benny said, "But they still work."

Grandfather, Henry, Jessie, and even Violet, who had been concentrating on her artwork, looked at Benny at the same time.

"What do you mean, Benny?" Henry asked.

Benny shrugged. "They still work."

"How do you know?"

"Because I closed them again," Benny replied. "Both of them. They clicked shut, and I couldn't open them."

His grandfather stopped rocking and leaned forward. "Are you sure about that?"

Benny nodded. "Uh-huh. I was just playing with them. I didn't think anyone would care because they were going to be thrown out anyway."

"I'm sure they ended up in the garbage," Jessie told her grandfather.

"Well, I think you should get them back and take a good look at them," Grandfather said. "If what Benny says is true, then something very strange is happening."

"I don't understand, Grandfather," Jessie said. "The locks were all banged up, as if someone had hit them with a hammer or something."

"Right, I remember when we were in the

mammal house. But if the thief really did break them open with force, then — "

"They shouldn't work anymore!" Henry said excitedly.

"And Benny's saying *both* locks still work," said Grandfather.

Benny nodded. "They both do, I'm sure of it."

"In that case," Grandfather said, "you should all take a look at them first thing in the morning. If Benny's right, then you've got a whole new mystery on your hands."

Jessie got up quickly. "I'll call Lindsey right now."

Early the next morning they returned to the little room in the mammal house where the black-footed ferrets had been stolen. Lindsey was so intrigued by what Jessie had told her on the phone that she and the Aldens got there a full hour before the zoo opened. Jordan Patterson, who received a call from Lindsey right after Jessie made her call, showed up, too.

Wearing a pair of yellow rubber gloves,

Jordan dug through the large plastic garbage can. The lock was at the bottom.

"We're very lucky," he said as he pulled it out. "The garbage is emptied every three days, and the janitor is very good at keeping on schedule. If we'd waited even a few more hours, this can would have a new bag in it, and this lock would be gone forever."

He brushed it off and handed it to Lindsey, who had brought a set of master keys from her office. The lock was, as Benny had said, closed. Lindsey tried to pull it open, but it held tight. Jessie patted her little brother on the shoulder. That part of his story had now been proven true.

Lindsey slipped the key into the hole and turned it. Sure enough, the lock, in spite of looking like it had been run over by a large truck, popped open. Lindsey tested it a few more times, and each time it worked fine.

"Incredible," Jordan said, scratching his head. "I just don't get it."

"We're not through yet, though," Lindsey said.

They all went over to the back room in

the Bird Barn. The cage lock there was still sitting on a table near the sink, waiting to be thrown out. Lindsey tested it, and the same thing happened.

"Yeah, it works fine," she said. "It's pretty banged up, but it works."

Henry said, "Wow."

"Now I'm really confused," Violet said.

"So am I," Benny added.

Jessie, on the other hand, was standing by herself near the condor cage, arms folded, deep in thought. She had a weird feeling that a big piece of the puzzle was close now — but she couldn't quite get *hold* of it. How frustrating!

It suddenly became clear when she looked one more time at the door to the condors' cage, in particular at the two little rings where the lock attached. One ring was on the door. The other was on the door frame. When the door was closed, the two rings were side-by-side, and the arm of the lock was slipped through both of them.

In a flash, everything made sense.

"Oh, my goodness!" she said, putting her

hands to her mouth. The others, who had been talking quietly among themselves, turned.

"What's the matter?" Lindsey asked.

Jessie smiled. "The locks! I think I know what happened!"

"Well, tell us," Jordan instructed.

She pointed to the rings on the cage. "See these?"

Henry nodded. "Yeah."

"They should be bent. If the thief really broke the locks off by force, like with a hammer or something, these little steel rings should be bent downward. If the thief hit the locks hard enough to break them open, there's no way these rings could've remained straight. They'd be all beaten up, too."

Jordan came over and examined the rings. "I think you're right, Jessie," he said slowly. "There isn't even a scratch on them."

"And I'll bet there isn't a scratch on the ones on the black-footed ferrets' cage, either." Jessie was really smiling big now. "That means the thief never broke the locks open. He or she had a key!"

Everyone froze. "A *key?*" Jordan asked. "That's impossible! Only the people who work here have keys, and I'm sure none of them would steal any animals."

"Are you positive?" Henry asked, but Lindsey was already nodding.

"Positive," Jordan said firmly.

"Yeah, I agree," Lindsey added quickly. "We've got a dynamite staff here. I'm just as sure as Jordan is."

"I had thought about that before," Violet mentioned, "about someone using a key, but I didn't think it was possible, either."

"And besides," Jordan went on, "the zoo-keepers only have keys to the buildings in which they work. At least, usually. The young woman who runs the mammal house can't get into the Bird Barn. Although some-times if one keeper is out sick, another will fill in for them."

Jessie nodded. "Whoever did it must have had a key. It's the only way to explain all this. The thief opened the . . ."

Her voice trailed off as her eyes went to the little cluster of nicks and dents in the floor.

"Of *course!*" she said loudly. Benny, whose attention had wandered toward a pair of parakeets, jumped.

"What now?" Henry asked.

"The little dents in the floor! Jordan, may I see that lock, please?"

She took it from him and turned it upside down. One edge was discolored by some chalky white powder. She knelt down and ran her finger over the dents on the cement floor. Sure enough, she found the exact same chalky powder.

"Okay," Jessie explained. "First the thief opened the locks with a key! Then, to make it *look* like he didn't have a key, he placed the locks on the floor" — she pointed to the dents — "and kept hitting them until they looked as though they'd been broken open. But the thief forgot to bend the little silver rings on the cage where the lock hangs."

"But now we've got an even bigger problem on our hands," Lindsey cut in. "We've got to figure out who has a key to all the cage door locks and who also happens to be an animal thief."

Jordan got to his feet again. "Well, there are only four people who have keys to all the cages," he said matter-of-factly. "Lindsey, myself, Mr. Colby, and Alan Parker, the head keeper. But again, I would stake everything I own that none of us is the thief."

"But . . . does anyone else have access to your keys?" Henry asked. "Anyone who can get a hold of them?"

"It's possible," Lindsey said. "I'll have to think about that."

"Hey," Henry said excitedly, "I'll bet the thief had keys to all the door locks, too."

"That's right!" Jessie agreed. "You thought that the window was probably too small! I'll bet the thief came right through the door!"

Violet added, "That's why the window was left open. The thief wanted us to think he or she came through there, too."

"But wasn't the window lock twisted and broken?" Benny asked.

"Only in here," Henry said. "In the mammal house it wasn't."

"A very inconsistent and absentminded thief," Jordan pointed out.

"Jordan, how old are these locks?" Jessie asked.

"Which ones?"

"All of them. The locks on the cages, the door locks . . ."

"Hmmm. I think they're all pretty old. We haven't bought new locks in a long time. No reason to, not as long as the ones we've already got are working okay. Why do you ask?"

"I had this idea — maybe the person who has the keys isn't someone who works here now, but did before."

Jordan's eyebrows rose. "I hadn't considered that."

Lindsey patted Jessie on the shoulder. "You're really batting a thousand today, kid."

Jordan said, "Jessie's right. Anyone who worked here in the past could've gotten copies made of all the keys. We've been open for nearly six years, and in that time

we've had a total of almost a hundred employees. Everyone from head keepers to
janitors. Any of them could, if they were
careful, get a copy made of each key."

Lindsey held hers up. There were about
fifty keys on one large silver hoop. "They're
too heavy to carry around all the time."

"Exactly," Jordan agreed.

"Someone could've sneaked into our offices while we were taking care of business
in the zoo somewhere, and taken off a few
keys at a time. We've got so many, we probably wouldn't even notice."

"Well, I'm going to get out a list of all
our past employees and go over the names
one by one," Jordan said. "Maybe someone
will stick out."

Just as he got to the door, he turned back
to the Aldens and said, "Lunch is on me today, kids. Who needs the police? You're the
best detectives around."

"Thanks, but the mystery is far from
solved," Henry pointed out. "There's still a
lot of work to do."

"Yep," Jordan agreed.

"All this thinking is making me hungry," said Benny. "Can we go to lunch early?"

Everyone laughed. "Sure," said Jessie.

"You three go on ahead," Henry told them. "I'll meet you at the food court. I just want to look around a little more."

As Henry was getting ready to head over to the food court about half an hour later, he spotted Beth, the intern, in the bushes along the outside of the Bird Barn. She was pushing against each window, apparently to see if they would open or not.

I wonder what she's up to, Henry thought.

He turned and headed in her direction, not really sure what he would say when he got to her. It didn't matter, though, because before he reached her, she turned and hurried off. Henry was sure she hadn't noticed him, but now he was more confused than ever. Was Beth trying to solve the mystery, too? Or was she part of it?

CHAPTER 6

A Waiting Game

Lindsey had to meet with Jordan again to discuss a few details. Then she caught up with the Aldens at the food court at noon for their free lunch.

"Jordan was really impressed with the things you came up with," she told Jessie as they ate.

Jessie smiled, almost embarrassed. "I'm just trying to help the zoo. Any of us could've thought up that stuff. It just happened to be me this time."

"Well, he really appreciates your help, all of you."

"Did he come up with any suspicious names on that employee list?" Henry asked.

"He didn't get a chance to look at it for very long. I looked it over, too, and no one jumped out at me." She tucked a loose strand of blond hair back behind her ear. "We've been lucky here, we really have. We've had a lot of good people on staff. Very few who didn't work out. When someone's left, it's usually been because he or she found a different job, went back to school, or moved. We haven't had to let too many people go."

"Of the ones you did let go, were any of them, you know . . . angry?" Henry asked.

Lindsey thought about it for a second, then shook her head. "No, not really. We've never had any nastiness, if that's what you mean. The few times we've had to let people go, it was because they just didn't seem to be working out. They cared for the animals very much, but they didn't have the knack for taking care of them properly. It takes a very special type of person to be a good zookeeper. Anyone can be a zookeeper, but only a few can be *good* zookeepers."

"Like you!" Benny said.

Lindsey blushed. "I'm not as good as I'd like to be, and there are people here who are better. Jordan's one of the best zookeepers in the world." She took another sip from her soda. "Jordan and Mr. Colby personally interview everyone who applies to work here. Between the two of them, they're very good at judging people. I still find it hard to believe someone who used to work here could be the thief."

"What are they going to do about the keys?" Jessie asked.

Violet nodded. "And what about the locks?"

Lindsey sighed. "I guess we're going to have to change all of them. The cage locks, the door locks. It's going to be very expensive."

"Mr. Colby won't be too happy about that, I'll bet," Jessie guessed.

"No, he certainly won't," Lindsey agreed. "But it's better than losing more animals. That would be a disaster."

Henry, who had been deep in thought for the last few minutes, said, "You know something? It might be better for you *not* to change any locks, at least not yet."

Lindsey stopped short of taking a bite from her sandwich. "Why would that be better?"

"Because you'll never catch the thief if you do."

"What do you mean?"

"Look, if you change all the locks now, and the thief tries to take some more animals, he or she will know you've figured out what's going on. Then that person will disappear for good, and you'll never get the ferrets or the condors back."

"Okay. . . ."

"So leave everything the way it is for now, let the thief think everything's fine. The thief has already made one big mistake with the "broken" locks. There's bound to be another, if we can just wait a little longer."

Jessie asked, "Has the night guard started yet?"

Lindsey shook her head. "No. He'll start on Monday."

"Maybe we can figure something out before then," Henry said. "Let's see . . . well, you know the thief is going after the endangered species. . . ."

"They're the most valuable," Lindsey pointed out, "so it makes sense."

"So what animal will be taken next?" Violet asked.

Lindsey frowned. "It gets much more serious now. I'm afraid this time the thief might go for the toads."

"Toads?" Jessie asked, surprised. "I thought there were lots of toads around."

"No," Lindsey said. "Some toads and frogs are very rare. And we have one of the rarest kinds in our program right now." She hesitated. "I think we'd better go talk to Dr. Hunziker. Come on."

They all met in the keeper's room behind the amphibian enclosures. It didn't take long for the Aldens to realize these back rooms all looked pretty much the same —bright lights, a cement floor, a long table, a pair of steel sinks, and a wall of supply shelves. There was something different in this room, however — the long table had rows and rows of plastic cups on it.

"What are they for?" Benny asked as the Aldens walked in with Jordan and Lindsey.

A man of about thirty with dark hair and glasses was going from cup to cup, sprinkling what looked like pink powder into each.

"This is Ray Hunziker, kids," Jordan said. "He's been the zoo's head reptile and amphibian keeper since the very first day it opened."

The Aldens and Dr. Hunziker exchanged hellos. Then Ray turned to Benny to answer his question. "They're nursery cups," he said with a warm smile.

"Nursery cups?"

"Yep. Come on over and have a look."

Benny peered into the first cup and saw something moving in the water. It was a little black oval with a squiggly tail.

"Is that . . . ?"

"A tadpole?" Ray asked.

"Yeah. . . ."

"Sure is."

"Wow!"

The others gathered around, looking into the other cups. Each one contained about two inches of clean water and a single tadpole.

"How long until they're big?" Benny asked.

"Oh, about six months. In a year they'll be full-grown."

"What kind of toads are these?" Violet asked.

"These are Wyoming toads," Ray told her. "They're truly endangered. There are none left in the wild at all."

"None at all?" asked Violet.

"None. Only four zoos keep them. They are the last of their kind."

"I don't remember you saying anything about them in the newspaper," Henry commented.

"Not yet," Jordan told them. "We'll want

to breed more of them first. Besides, if the thief got them, that would be a disaster not only for us, but for the whole species as well." He put a finger to his lips, as if telling someone to be quiet. "This is one of our top-secret projects, so don't say a word to anyone."

"We won't," Benny assured him.

Lindsey walked to the next enclosure. "These are the poison-arrow frogs."

"They're cool," Benny said.

"But dangerous," Violet added. "If handled, they can cause painful skin rashes on humans."

"I guess a thief wouldn't want these," Henry guessed.

"No, that's not necessarily true," Lindsey said. "People like to collect them even though they're dangerous. They're very pretty, so that makes them desirable. You just have to know how to handle them properly."

Henry went back and looked at the Wyoming toad tadpoles again. "I like these little guys," he said. "Even if they're not pretty. I hope nothing happens to them."

"Does *anyone* know about them?" asked Jessie.

Lindsey looked very serious. "Some people do know," she said. "I'm still kind of worried."

The next morning, back at the house, the Aldens were eating breakfast together when the phone rang. Grandfather answered it. "Oh, no!" the children heard him say. "I'll send them right over." He hung up and turned to his grandchildren.

"You kids better get down to the zoo."

"Why? What's wrong?" Violet asked.

"The toads?" Benny asked, already fearing the answer.

Grandfather nodded sadly. "The thief paid another visit last night. Lindsey really needs your help now."

The Aldens hurried down to the zoo and headed straight for Amphibian Hall. Lindsey, Jordan, and Dr. Hunziker were already there—and the long table that held all the nursery cups yesterday was empty.

"It's not quite as bad as it seems," Dr.

Hunziker said. "I was so worried last night that I moved some of the tadpoles out of here. But I didn't have time to get all of them. I had to get home." He shrugged. "So at least the thief didn't get all of them."

"But look what else was stolen," Lindsey said, pointing to the poison-arrow frog enclosure. It was empty.

"Every one," Lindsey replied. "All fifteen of them."

"And the lock to the panel?" Jessie asked.

"Over on the table," Lindsey said, pointing. Like the others, it looked like it had been run over by a truck.

"And the marks — " Jessie began to ask, but Lindsey already knew the question. She pointed to a spot on the floor a few feet in front of the main door.

"They're right there."

Sure enough, there was a little cluster of dents and scratches where the thief had beaten the lock to make it look as though it had been broken open.

"Was any food stolen this time?" Violet wanted to know.

"Impossible to tell," Jordan answered.

"Why?" Violet asked.

"Because poison-arrow frogs eat tiny crickets," Jordan told her. "See that garbage can over there? The one with the lid on it?" He nodded toward a big blue can by the sinks.

"It's full of tiny crickets. Go have a look."

Violet went over, her brothers and sister behind, and carefully lifted the lid. Inside were thousands of tiny brown crickets. There were also a few apple slices and a wet sponge in a glass bowl.

"Wow," she said. "Look at all of them."

"We breed those, too," Jordan told her. "They're easy to breed, and certainly not endangered. But if the thief took a bunch, how could we tell? We don't keep count."

"Lindsey, do you think it will turn out to be Beth, the intern, who's the thief?" Jessie asked.

"It's a possibility. She *has* said many times that her collection of pets at home gets better care than the animals do here. Maybe she's taking them because she thinks she can give them a better home. And she does have access to most of the rooms and could get keys from the other keepers."

"There's something else," said Jessie. "She drives a van. I saw her getting into it in the parking lot."

"A van? Why would that make her a suspect?" asked Henry.

"I guess alone it wouldn't make her a suspect," said Jessie, "but if she did steal the animals . . . well, the ferrets wouldn't have been a problem, but that van of hers would sure have come in handy for those condors."

"True . . ." said Lindsey.

"I saw her near the windows of the Bird Barn not too long ago," Henry added. "She was pushing on them, like she was checking to see which ones opened and which ones didn't."

Lindsey nodded. "Interesting, very interesting. Maybe I'll say something to her."

"And what about the man in the bright shirt?" Benny said. "The one Violet and I saw taking notes. Could he be the thief?"

Henry filled Lindsey in about the new suspect and they all agreed to watch out for him at the zoo.

Darren Colby came into the room at that moment, dressed in his usual dark suit and tie.

"I just heard about the stolen frogs and toads," he said to Jordan, ignoring everyone else. "I'm sorry, Jordan, but that's three strikes. I'm afraid the breeding program has to be stopped."

"Oh, no!" Violet said.

"I'm sorry," Mr. Colby went on, "but the zoo is losing too much money, and if the public finds out it will make us look bad. Nobody wants to come to a zoo that's losing all its animals."

"What if we find them again?" Jessie asked. "What if we catch the thief?"

"If you kids can do that," Mr. Colby said, "then we're back in business. You have my word."

Benny smiled. "We'll do it. You'll see!"

"I hope so," Mr. Colby replied.

CHAPTER 7

Mrs. Donovan Remembers

Lindsey came to the Aldens' house for dinner that night. But in spite of the delicious roast chicken, no one was very hungry.

"This is such a nightmare," Lindsey was saying, chin in hand. "I can't believe the thief got all those frogs and toads. Whoever the person is, they're very clever." She sighed. "I wonder if we'll ever catch the thief."

"I was thinking about something. . . ." Violet said, picking at her cake with her fork. "Something about those poison-arrow frogs."

"What about them?" Lindsey asked.

"If the thief took them, wouldn't he or she get a rash?"

"Probably," Lindsey replied. "But all he'd have to do to avoid that is wear rubber gloves. Like the ones used in the kitchen."

"But," Violet continued, "if the thief was meaning to steal only the Wyoming toads, why would he or she bring gloves?"

"Hey, that's right," Jessie added. "The thief obviously meant to take the Wyoming toads because they were the animals featured in the breeding program. The thief probably saw the poison-arrow frogs and thought, *Hey, they're pretty. Maybe I'll take those, too.* Because the thief wasn't expecting to take the poison-arrow frogs, he or she wouldn't have brought gloves along. He would have picked up the poison frogs with bare hands. I think the thief has made the mistake we've been hoping for."

Lindsey started nodding. "You know something? I think you're right."

"If that's what happened," Violet said, "when would the rash appear?"

Lindsey looked at her watch. "It would be in full bloom by now. It's been twelve hours at least, and it takes only about eight for the rash to surface."

"Is it possible the thief could have developed the rash and gone to the local hospital?" Jessie wondered. "Would it be worth it to call over there and ask if anyone came in with such a rash?"

Henry shook his head and cut in with, "If I were the thief and I had a weird rash caused by some animals I'd stolen, I certainly wouldn't want anyone to know about it. A doctor would want to know how the rash was caused. Right, Grandfather?"

Grandfather Alden nodded. "Of course. The doctor would have to know the cause, or else the rash couldn't be treated properly."

"And the thief wouldn't dare tell the truth," Jessie continued. "Painful or not, the thief would have to keep quiet."

"I had a skin rash once," Benny added. "It sure hurt!"

"How'd that happen?" Lindsey asked.

"Poison ivy," Benny told her. "It was all over me, and it itched like crazy. I think I got it from playing with Watch in the woods." Benny looked over at his beloved dog. "He didn't get it, though."

Everyone laughed. "Dogs don't get rashes from poison ivy," Jessie said. "Right, Lindsey?"

"Nope. They're very lucky that way. So did you have to go to the hospital, Benny?"

Henry said, "No, we just took him to Dr. Hughes's office."

"And he gave Benny a shot?" Lindsey asked.

"No. He wrote a prescription for this really strong cream. We had to go to the drug store to g — "

Henry stopped in midsentence. He and Lindsey looked at each each other.

"Hey!" he said.

"Hey!" she said back.

"Are you thinking what I'm thinking?" he asked.

"I think so," Lindsey said.

Grandfather smiled. "I think I am, too."

"Me, too!" Jessie said.

"And me," Violet added.

Benny, who suddenly felt left out, cried, "I don't know what anyone's talking about!"

"Sorry, Benny!" Henry said. "The drugstore! That might be the answer! If the thief had a rash and didn't want anyone to know about it, he or she could go to a drugstore to get medicine." Henry looked around at the others. "That's what you were all thinking, right?" Everyone nodded.

"Oh," Benny said. "I get it."

Lindsey got up, full of energy again. "So where do we start?" she asked. "There must be half a dozen drugstores in this area."

"I guess we might as well start with the closest one," said Grandfather. "That would be Donovan's on the village square."

The Aldens and Lindsey drove to Donovan's Drugstore in the center of Greenfield and spoke with Mrs. Donovan, the pharmacist there. They did not want to ask personal questions about her customers, so they asked in a general way about how a serious rash might be treated without a doctor's prescription.

"Well," she said, "there are a lot of strong creams on the market nowadays. Used to be you'd need a prescription for them." She went on to name a few of the most popular brands. "As a matter of fact," she offered, "I recall a young man came in today and bought three different creams. He had a nasty rash. Said it was poison ivy, but it didn't look like poison ivy to me."

Lindsey and the Aldens stood very still for a moment, not believing their good luck.

"You said he was a young man?" Grandfather asked.

"Yes, a polite young man," Mrs. Donovan continued. "On the thin side. I remember him because he wore a Boston Red Sox cap and they're my favorite team. That, and he had the bluest eyes I've ever seen."

At this last remark, Lindsey looked sharply at James Alden.

"Are you children working on some kind of research project?" Mrs. Donovan asked.

"Sort of," Henry answered, "and I promise when we are done with it, we will tell you all about it. But right now we're kind of in a hurry."

The Aldens and Lindsey thanked Mrs. Donovan for her help and left the store. As soon as they were out on the sidewalk, the Aldens turned to Lindsey.

"Well, I guess that rules out Beth," said Henry.

"And our suspect with the bright shirts," said Benny. "He definitely was not skinny."

"Does the young man Mrs. Donovan described sound familiar?" Grandfather asked Lindsey.

"Yeah, I think he does," Lindsey said. "I don't remember his name, but I remember his blue eyes and the baseball cap. I think we still have his file at the office. We keep records of all our employees, both past and present. I'll check into it first thing in the morning. I assume you guys will be with me?"

"We wouldn't miss it for the world," Henry assured her.

CHAPTER 8

A Surprise Visitor

The Aldens sat in Lindsey's office the next morning, watching her at her desk as she flipped through a set of files. Bright beams of sunlight slanted through the window, and sparrows chirped in the trees outside.

"Here it is," she said, pulling out one folder and setting the rest aside. "Brian Grady. I am sure of it now."

She opened the folder and laid it flat on her desk. The Aldens gathered around.

As soon as Benny saw the picture

of Grady attached to the first page, he gasped.

"I wasn't sure by what Mrs. Donovan said, but now I'm positive," Benny said. "I've seen him before!"

"You have?" Jessie asked.

"Yeah, in the Reptile Range. He was there a few days ago! I'm sure it was him! He was wearing a Red Sox hat!"

"That's his favorite team," Lindsey said. "I remember he talked about them a lot. The Red Sox and animals, his two great loves."

"What do you think he was doing in the Reptile Range?" Violet asked.

"Probably getting some ideas as to which animals he would take next," Lindsey guessed.

"And he used to work here?" Jessie asked.

Lindsey nodded. "Yes, but only for a few months. He cared a great deal about the animals, but he wasn't a very good keeper. That's why we had to let him go. He kept forgetting to feed certain animals or clean their cages. Some of the other keepers had to do a lot of his work for him. He was very absentminded."

Henry said, "Wow, just like with the rings on the cages. He forgot about those, too."

"Exactly," Lindsey agreed. "We gave him the normal ninety-day trial period, but after that we had to replace him. He was very sad, I remember, but not mad or anything like that."

She looked back down at the file, read a few lines, then smiled. "Says here he lives on Pittman Avenue."

Violet's eyes widened. "That's near Donovan's Drugstore!"

Lindsey nodded. "You got it. Kids, I think we've caught our thief!"

"Yes!" Benny said triumphantly.

Lindsey looked at his picture again, then shook her head. "He wasn't a great animal keeper, but he was a nice person. I never would've figured him for a criminal." Then she added, "Well, at least we know now that it wasn't Beth."

"I'll bet she was conducting a little investigation of her own when I saw her sneaking around the Bird Barn," Henry said.

Lindsey nodded. "You're probably right."

"So what do we do now?" Jessie wondered.

"I think it's time to call the police," Lindsey said. "Wouldn't you agree?"

"We've certainly got enough evidence to make him a prime suspect," Henry said.

"Yes, we certainly do," Lindsey replied. She reached over and picked up the phone. "Okay, here goes."

She began tapping in the numbers, but before she finished, a new voice said, "There's no need for you to do that, Ms. Taylor."

Everyone turned, then froze in complete surprise.

Standing in the doorway, holding a big plastic bag containing the missing poison-arrow frogs in one hand and a bucket containing the Wyoming toad tadpoles in another, was Brian Grady. There were white gauze bandages wrapped around his hands, and he looked miserably unhappy.

His voice was shaky. "I can't do this anymore," he said. "I feel just awful about what I've done." He crossed the room and handed the bag to Lindsey. The frogs and toad tadpoles appeared to be in good health and color. "Here, put these back where they belong, please."

"How's the rash?" Lindsey asked first.

"It's getting better, slowly. But it doesn't hurt half as much as thinking about what I've done."

"Yeah, well, you're lucky, Brian. These are the Aldens, and they're just about the best young detectives in the world. Another few hours and they would've caught you anyway, with the help of the local police. Now, what do you know about the condors and the ferrets?"

"I . . . I don't . . . they're not with me anymore," he replied, almost choking on the words.

"What do you mean?" Lindsey asked. She sounded angry. "It would be best if you told us what's been going on. You're not in a very good spot right now."

Brian was nodding. "Yes, yes, I know. Of course I'll tell you everything." He sat down and buried his face in his bandaged hands.

"Okay," he began after a long breath, "here's the whole thing from the start. A few weeks ago I received a call from some guy. He didn't say his name, and his voice didn't sound familiar. He asked me if I wanted to make some good money doing work with animals. Of course I was interested. He sort of laughed and said, 'I figured you would be.' The funny thing is, I hadn't had a job in almost two months and I was getting low on cash, so he called at just the right time. I was falling behind on my bills. I think I would've done just about any work at that point, but when this guy mentioned animals, I thought it was a dream come true."

"So . . ."

"So then he started talking about the

breeding program, said he'd been following it in the newspapers. He said he knew I used to work here, but that I'd been . . . well, fired. I don't know how he knew. I guess he must've visited a few times and seen me here, then visited again and realized I was gone."

"So what else did he say?" Henry asked.

"He wanted to know if I could still get into the zoo. You know, with the keys. I said no, I had to give my set back when I left. He asked if I'd made any copies, and I told him I hadn't. By this point I was getting a little nervous. His questions were kind of . . . I don't know, weird."

"But you kept talking to him anyway," Jessie pointed out.

Brian nodded and looked down shamefully. "Yeah. Like I said, I was in a tight spot for money."

"What happened next?"

"Well, he didn't seem to be too bothered by the fact that I didn't have keys. He said, 'Oh, I was just wondering.' Then he finally got to the point — he wanted to know if I'd be willing to take some of the animals from the zoo. I said, 'You mean steal them?' I was shocked, really. I just couldn't believe it. But he said, 'Yes, steal them. Would you do that?' I told him no, I wouldn't. And I meant it, too. But then he said, 'Not even for five hundred dollars per animal?' "

Brian looked back up helplessly. "I still didn't want to do it, but . . . five hundred bucks is a lot to me. It would help me out a great deal. So I agreed."

"How was everything arranged?" Henry cut in.

"The guy said I should go out to that little park on the other side of town. You know the one? Over by Gallagher's Pond?"

Benny said, "Sure, we bring Watch over there all the time. He's our dog."

Brian smiled a little. "The guy said I should look for a large rock underneath a fir tree about a hundred feet from the pond's footbridge. Behind it there would be a plastic bag containing some keys and a note. It wasn't hard to find. There's only about ten fir trees in the whole park, and only one has a big boulder at the base."

"What did the note say?" Lindsey asked.

"It told me which animals I was supposed to take, and which building they were in."

Jessie said, "And what about the keys?"

"They were copies," Brian told her. "I'm sure of it. Each one was brand-new; the teeth were real sharp."

"Did the note say anything else?"

Brian nodded. "It said that once I opened one of the cage locks, I should — "

"Beat it up to make it look as though you'd broken it open?" Jessie asked.

"How did you know that?" Brian wondered.

"We figured it out on our own," Henry replied.

"I told you, they're great detectives," Lindsey reminded him.

Brian nodded. "Wow, I guess so. Well, the note said to do that, and that I had to return the keys, along with the animals, each time. I was supposed to leave the animals behind the same rock, always at some time during the night. The note said I should then leave immediately, and that if I hung around to see who'd pick them up, I'd be very sorry." He shivered. "I didn't like the sound of that."

"When you left the animals, was the money waiting for you?" Jessie asked.

"Yes. I just took it and ran. I really wasn't interested in finding out who would come to take the animals. I know this sounds hard to believe, but I wanted nothing more to do with that person."

"And that was it?"

"That was it. It was really very simple. A few days later, the guy called again. The first time it was for the ferrets, then the condors, and then the toads. I didn't even plan on taking the poison frogs, either. The ones that caused this," he said, holding his hands up. "They were just so . . . so beautiful. I wanted them for myself, and I wasn't thinking. I figured I could take good care of them . . . but I was wrong, obviously. I took the wrong food for the ferrets, for example."

"And the voice on the phone never sounded familiar to you?" Jessie asked.

"No."

"But it's easy to disguise your voice over the phone, anyway," Henry pointed out, and everyone agreed.

Brian put his hands on his knees and let out a long sigh. "That's the whole story. I guess I'm in deep trouble, huh? Well, it's better than living with the guilt. I never even spent the money I got. It's still sitting on my dresser in the same envelopes!"

Lindsey shook her head. "You have no idea at all who the person was or what he might have done with the animals?"

"Not a clue. I guess he sold them. They were worth a lot of money, I'm sure."

Lindsey nodded sadly. "Yes, they were. Brian, I don't know what we're supposed to do with you now. You've committed some very serious crimes."

"I know that, and I wouldn't blame you

for turning me in. I'd do anything to get those animals back, but I've already told you everything I know. You might as well call the police and have them come get me. I deserve it."

"Are you sure about that?" Lindsey asked. "Because I know that's what Jordan and Mr. Colby will want to do when I tell them you're here."

Brian paused, then nodded. "Yeah, I'm sure. I won't feel better about myself until I start paying my debt."

Lindsey reach for the phone. "Okay. . . ."

For the second time that morning, she began dialing the number of the local police department, then got interrupted before she had a chance to finish.

"Wait!" Henry said, putting his hand up. "I just thought of something!"

Lindsey hung up the phone. "What?"

Henry smiled. "Maybe Brian *can* help us!"

"Huh?"

Henry turned to him. "You're still supposed to drop off these tadpoles, right?"

"Well . . . yeah, sure. I'm *supposed* to, but I'm not going to."

"Sure you are," Henry said.

Brian looked over at Lindsey, then back at Henry. "I am?"

"Uh-huh. And after you leave, we're going to catch us a criminal!" Henry said delightedly. "When the guy shows up, he's going to find a lot more than a bag of toad tadpoles waiting for him. Everyone get the idea?"

Lindsey smiled. "Yeah, I do."

"But we'd better not tell Jordan or Mr. Colby about this," Henry warned. "They might not go for it."

"We'll try it first," Lindsey agreed.

Henry rubbed his hands together. "Okay, here's what we're going to do. . . ."

CHAPTER 9

To Catch a Thief

When Grandfather Alden heard of the plan to catch the mysterious caller, he insisted on being part of it, just to be safe.

Shortly after dark, he and the children, plus Lindsey, took their places. They hid in a little cluster of trees about fifty feet from the fir tree with the large rock at the base. They were far enough away to see what was going on without running the risk of being noticed.

At precisely eight o'clock, Brian came

walking down the main path, as planned, but with a plastic bag filled with nothing but water.

Brian set the bag down behind the rock, picked up the envelope of money, then returned the way he came, careful not to look back. Having done that, his part in the plan was over. He and the others had agreed that he shouldn't hang around, just in case the mystery man was watching him. He was also careful not to give any hints as to where Lindsey and the Aldens were hiding. He was to act like this was an ordinary "drop," just like the last two. It was important for the mystery man to believe everything was going normally.

After Brian disappeared, the park fell silent. A few crickets chirped in the tall grass bordering Gallagher's Pond, and some peepers trilled in the low bushes. The moon burned bright in the cloudless sky, casting everything in a soothing white glow. The air was cool and still.

After the first hour passed, everyone began to get a little worried.

"I wonder if we scared him off," Jessie whispered. "I wonder if he knew somehow."

"Anything's possible," Grandfather answered. "Whoever this man is, he's been pretty clever so far."

"I say we wait another hour, at the most," Lindsey told them.

"I agree," Grandfather replied.

As it turned out, the guest of honor showed up about fifteen minutes later.

He left a smaller trail and walked out onto the main path. He was a large person, dressed in a dark overcoat and a dark hat. He kept his collar turned up and his head low, making it impossible to see his face. He looked around cautiously, which wasn't surprising. The Aldens also wore dark clothes, and they'd made a wise decision — the mystery man looked directly at them but didn't see them. Once he seemed sure he was alone, he headed for the big rock under the fir tree.

"Okay, let's go," Grandfather Alden said in a whisper. "And remember — *quietly*."

The Alden party filed out of the woods

with their grandfather a good ten steps in the lead. The mystery man was already at the big rock, reaching behind it to claim his latest prize. By the time he brought the bag out and realized it contained nothing but water, Grandfather Alden was already behind him.

"What in the world — ?"

"Hold it right there, my friend," Grandfather said firmly. The rest of his team gathered around. "Sorry, but I'm afraid this little game of yours is over."

The man remained frozen for a moment. Then his shoulders sagged and his head drooped. He turned to face the people who had captured him. As he did, his identity was finally revealed.

Violet gasped. Benny's eyes grew enormous. Jessie's hands went to her mouth.

And Lindsey said in a truly disappointed voice, "Oh, Mr. Colby, how could you?"

Back at the Alden home the following evening, Grandfather held a huge celebration dinner. Jordan and Lindsey came, and so did Brian, who wanted to apologize to Jordan in person.

After dinner, Jordan took Brian home, and Danny Fischer, a reporter from the local newspaper, arrived. A short, strongly built, enthusiastic young man, Danny wanted to cover the story of the zoo thefts for the local paper. As soon as he walked into the living room, Benny jumped up. Benny remembered him from the food court a few days ago. Now that the mystery was over, the young reporter was eager to gather the exciting details of this intriguing chapter in town history.

"I know you," Benny said. "You're the man with the bright shirts! You were taking notes at the zoo!"

"Right you are," said Danny with a laugh, and he introduced himself to the Aldens.

He sat on the living room couch with his notepad. Lindsey was next to him, the children spread out on the floor. Watch, as always, snoozed peacefully nearby. Grandfather sat in his easy chair with his eyes closed, feet up, and his hands folded across his chest.

"So Darren Colby was going to do what with the animals?" Danny asked, his pen at the ready.

"He was going to have them returned to the wild," Jessie said. "Which, according to Lindsey, isn't the worst thing that could have happened to them."

Lindsey nodded. "We all thought he was going to sell them. That would have been truly terrible."

"He said he didn't want to hurt them," Benny pointed out.

The reporter shook his head. "It doesn't sound like he did."

Lindsey said, "No, Mr. Colby did some bad things, but he didn't try to hurt any of the animals. Thank goodness he wasn't that kind of a person."

"And why exactly did he do this in the first place?" Danny asked.

"Money," Lindsey answered quickly. "It's always been about money with him."

"I . . . I don't understand," Danny said. "If he wasn't planning on selling the animals, then why would he have done all this for the money?"

"He wanted to spend the money that they put toward the animals on building a small amusement park at the zoo instead," Henry told him. "Rides, games, a candy shop, stuff like that."

Lindsey nodded. "His way of thinking was this: Spending a lot of money on endangered species would bring in a few more visitors. But putting together an amusement park would bring in a *lot* more visitors, and more visitors meant more money. He and Jordan had argued about this quite a bit. Mr. Colby was only thinking of ways to make more money. And he planned to use the insurance money from the stolen animals to help pay for the building of the amusement park. Jordan wanted instead to make a little less money, but do more for the animals. That's how it always was with those two — Mr. Colby only thought about money, Jordan only thought about animals."

Danny said, "So . . . Colby wanted to make it look like the animals were being stolen because . . ."

"He needed a real excuse to shut down the breeding program," Jessie finished. "Then he could say to Jordan, 'You see what a bad idea that was?' Then Jordan wouldn't have any way to argue against his amusement park idea anymore."

"And his plan almost worked, too," Lindsey said. "After he shut down the program, we thought that was it for sure. We figured the rest of the endangered species would be returned to the zoos where we first got them, and they'd start building the park right away."

Danny scribbled all this down on his pad. "But you kids came along and figured everything out, right?"

Henry nodded. "I guess so."

"Don't be so modest, Henry," Grandfather said, eyes still closed. "My grandchildren are the finest detectives around. I pity anyone who tries to commit a crime around here. They don't stand a chance."

Everyone laughed. "It makes for a great story, I'll tell you that," Danny assured them. "And I'm going to put it all in, too."

"Well, you don't have to do that," Jessie said. "We were just glad to help."

Hearing this warmed her grandfather's heart.

"So what happened to all the other animals that were first taken?" Danny continued. "The ferrets and the condors?"

Violet giggled. "They were in Mr. Colby's house. They made a mess."

"A mess?" Danny asked.

Lindsey smiled. "I don't know if you've ever been around ferrets, Danny, but they're very mischievous animals. They love to hide things, chew things, tear things. Mr. Colby tried to keep them in their cages, but every now and then he had to take them out so he could do a cleaning. Of course, having no experience with animals or animal care, his attempts were always disastrous. The ferrets would scurry off and hide, and then Mr. Colby would find holes in his clothes or little things would be missing. They are very naughty creatures."

"The ferrets were pretty hungry because they had the wrong kind of food," Benny said. "I felt really sorry for them."

"And what about the condors?"

"He kept them in his cellar. They were very loud and very mean sometimes. They're actually kind of dangerous and should be handled only by experts. He got a nasty scratch on his arm from one of them."

"But the animals are okay now?" Danny asked.

"Yes," Benny piped in. "I checked them myself."

Lindsey smiled. "Benny was my assistant when I gave them a checkup after we got them back. All the animals were in good health and happy to be home again."

"That's wonderful," Danny said, writing it all down. "So what happens to Mr. Colby now?"

"He's not a partner at the zoo anymore," Henry said.

"And that's probably best," Grandfather added. "I don't think he's cut out for zoo work."

Lindsey offered some further details: "He's agreed to sell his part of the zoo, and in return no charges will be pressed against him."

"But won't the next partner be the same way?" Danny asked. "Won't he be a businessman, too?"

Jessie smiled and shook her head. "I doubt it. Jordan's the new partner."

Danny looked surprised. "You're kidding!"

Lindsey said, "Nope. Jordan has decided to run the zoo entirely by himself from now on. He had to take out a big bank loan to buy out Mr. Colby's share, but I think in the long run he'll be a lot happier. He said he learned a lot from Mr. Colby about how to run a business, and he thinks he can do it on his own. We'll all help him, of course. It'll be tight for a while, but we'll manage."

"And we'll help, too!" Benny pointed out.

"That's right," Lindsey said, looking at the little boy. "Benny and his family have agreed to come by every now and then and help out with some of the little tasks. That'll certainly save us some money."

"Well, that's really terrific," Danny said, still scribbling. "This is going to make one fabulous story. Finally, what about the kid who actually took the animals? Will he be charged by the police?"

Lindsey said, "No. Jordan came up with a better idea. . . ."

The Aldens fixed their attention on her. Even Grandfather opened his eyes. Lindsey had announced right before the reporter came that Jordan had something special in mind for Brian, but she wanted to wait until just the right moment to reveal it.

"He's going to rehire Brian as an apprentice keeper," she said.

Violet smiled. "That's wonderful!"

"Good for him," Grandfather said.

"He didn't really seem like he had his heart in being a thief anyway," Henry joked.

"No, he didn't," Lindsey said. "He wants to take care of animals. He's a keeper by nature, he just has to learn to be more responsible. So we're going to give him some training and we'll see how he does."

"What did he do with the money he got from Mr. Colby for taking the animals?" Danny asked.

"The money goes back to the zoo," Jessie answered.

Danny wrote a few more lines, then closed the cover of his notepad.

"Well, this has been one incredible story, I must say," Danny told them. "The best one I've ever covered. I don't know how I'm going to top it."

"Oh, just keep an eye on my grandchildren," Grandfather Alden advised, "and I'm sure you'll have lots to write about. They'll make you famous!"

Henry put his hand on Benny's shoulder. "Maybe we should tell you about what happened to Benny right before he saw you at the food court that day. Now, that was really news!"

Danny's face brightened with anticipation. "What? What happened?"

"I lost my appetite for a few minutes!" Benny said, and everyone burst out laughing.

"And around here," Grandfather added, "that really is big news."

GERTRUDE CHANDLER WARNER discovered when she was teaching that many readers who like an exciting story could find no books that were both easy and fun to read. She decided to try to meet this need, and her first book, *The Boxcar Children*, quickly proved she had succeeded.

Miss Warner drew on her own experiences to write the mystery. As a child she spent hours watching trains go by on the tracks opposite her family home. She often dreamed about what it would be like to set up housekeeping in a caboose or freight car — the situation the Alden children find themselves in.

When Miss Warner received requests for more adventures involving Henry, Jessie, Violet, and Benny Alden, she began additional stories. In each, she chose a special setting and introduced unusual or eccentric characters who liked the unpredictable.

While the mystery element is central to each of Miss Warner's books, she never thought of them as strictly juvenile mysteries. She liked to stress the Aldens' independence and resourcefulness and their solid New England devotion to using up and making do. The Aldens go about most of their adventures with as little adult supervision as possible — something else that delights young readers.

Miss Warner lived in Putnam, Connecticut, until her death in 1979. During her lifetime, she received hundreds of letters from girls and boys telling her how much they liked her books.